B & B

BED AND BOYFRIEND

KIM MATOS

FOR STEFAN AND ANDREA

LOVE IS A BEAUTIFUL THING

JEN RADFORD

CONTENTS

INTRODUCTION

This book is a short story of a young girl whose only love was her bed until she found a boyfriend and other stories.

CONTACT ME

Click here to join my Reader's group and your free book "COUGAR HUSBAND AND OTHER STORIES" - It will be delivered to your inbox.You will also be kept up to date about other giveaways coming up soon.

CHAPTER I

Bed & Boyfriend

My parents were wonderful to us, but terrible to each other. It came from both sides. It would always start as something small, but then one of them would bring up the past. And soon they'd be fighting over their entire history. It was mostly a lot of loudness. I have distinct memories of doors being broken and objects being thrown. My older brother would bring me into his room and tell me stories to distract me. If I was all alone I'd just hide under the covers. But even at that age I knew what I wanted. And I made a promise to myself: my children will never go through this. Greg and I started dating our freshman year of college. We were so young. I had no idea how to be in a healthy relationship. Every time we got in a fight, I'd say it was over. Because that's all I knew. My parents were always threatening divorce. But Greg kept saying: 'We're not going to do that. I'm staying right here.' He had that kind of maturity—even at the age of eighteen. I was the immature one. I'd say the most horrible things to him: 'I hate you,' and things like that. Things I'd heard my parents say. But he never hurt me back. Not once. I don't ever tell people that, because it doesn't seem possible. But we've been together twenty years, and he's never said anything hurtful. There have been some challenging times. We're raising two daughters. We have a beautiful son in heaven. So we've had our share of arguments, but I've never been insulted. I've never been shamed. He doesn't bring up things I've done wrong in the past. I always joke with him that I'm the crappy person. I'm the one who lashes out. I'm the one who talks about people, and judges, and puts my foot in my mouth. He doesn't react like me. He responds. And he's made me so much better. Through twenty years of watching him respond, I've improved a little bit each day. Sometimes I wish that I could go back and comfort my younger self, hiding under the covers, crying herself to sleep. I'd tell her that it's hard to believe—but one day she'll be grateful for what happened to her. Because in a few years she's going to meet someone wonderful. And because of everything she's been through—she'll know just how wonderful he is."

CHAPTER II

He Stole My Night

One of my earliest memories is sitting in a sand box and watching the other kids play. I could see their mouths moving but couldn't hear what they were talking about. They seemed so happy. And I desperately wanted to participate. But my deafness kept me in a glass cage. I was never able to verbally speak. And whenever I tried to reach out—I'd be forgotten quickly. During recess I'd sit alone and read my books, because it hurt too much to look at the other kids. In high school I had an interpreter who predicted I'd never marry. She said that disabled people were too much of a burden for abled people. It was a casual remark for her, but I never forgot it. And the few flings I had as a teenager only reinforced that belief. None of the guys I dated learned sign language. They didn't even try. I think they viewed dating a deaf girl as more of a novelty than anything. And every time it didn't work out, I was left feeling lonelier. I went to college two hours away. Which wasn't far—but it was far for me. And I first met Stuart in my education class. He tried to say 'hello' that very first day, but I accidentally ignored him. I think he figured out the reason once my interpreter showed up. But he kept smiling at me, and a few days later he slid me a photo with a note on the back and his email address. I spent a lot of time looking at that photo, waffling back and forth about whether I should contact him. But finally I decided there was nothing to lose. We began spending time together outside of class. We'd communicate by writing back and forth in a notebook. I learned all about his life. And he learned about mine. After a few months of this, I started to have hope—maybe he was actually interested in my thoughts. Maybe he liked me for me. One night we were watching a scary movie in my dorm room. We were writing back and forth, laughing at the cheesy scenes, when suddenly Stuart's face grew serious. He wrote that he needed to tell me something. My heart sank. I thought: This is where he tells me that I'm a lot of fun, but my deafness is a dealbreaker. But he looked me in the eyes, took a deep breath, and haltingly began to sign: 'Will. You. Be. My. Girlfriend?'"

CHAPTER III

Electric Love

I'd just gotten out of a ten-year relationship. I didn't want to date. I didn't even know how to date. But my friend Marla was really working on me. For months she was trying to get me to go on a blind date with her friend Kate. She'd talk about her. She'd show me pictures. But I was scared, so I'd find any excuse not to go through with it. She seemed too wholesome. She was from the Midwest. And worst of all—she had a kid. I was childless for a reason. I'd had a difficult childhood. My father was an alchoholic and sexually abusive. Two of my siblings died by suicide. And somehow I'd internalized that it was my fault. I had a belief that children ruined their parents' lives. But I agreed to meet Kate any-way. We met at a park in the middle of a rare March snowstorm. The snow was really coming down, but we still walked for three miles around a lake. Kate talks a lot when she's nervous, so I heard her whole life story. Being a mother was such an important part of her life. And she was determined to have another child. She'd just gotten to the end of a long adoption process, but at the last minute, the girl's father wouldn't let a lesbian adopt her child. I listened to Kate's heartbreak, and her determination, and I couldn't help falling in love. After a few months of dating, I was al-lowed to meet her son. And he was wonderful. But another child? A baby? I tried to talk her out of it. And she tried to meet me in the middle. She did her best to not want another child. But even-tually she told me that it was going to happen, and I needed to make a decision. I took a two-week trip to Bali for a yoga retreat. I sat in daily meditation. And one morning I had a vision of a young girl in my lap. I could feel her warmth against my body. I seemed happy. And she seemed happy. It was such a feeling of peace. And there was Kate—smiling at us both. By the time I opened my eyes, I had made my decision. But unbeknownst to me, Kate had also made a decision. She needed a partner who was fully committed. So she came to the airport ready to break up with me. But she didn't have a chance. Because the moment I got off the plane, I told her: 'Let's get married. I'm ready to be a mother.'"

CHAPTER IV

Accidental Wedding

It drove my mom mental. The minute I got home, I was right in front of the computer. But video games were the only place I fit in. I was never very popular in school—even though I wanted to be. But things were different online. People respected the way I played. Back then it was mostly Warcraft III—and I was good at it. I wasn't ranked at the top or anything, but I had over 1800 wins. Most people didn't even believe I was a girl. One night I was randomly paired with a player named SirFishingKill, and we stomped the other team. We overran their bases with a giant army of crypt fiends and frost wyrms. Then we played another game. And another. Until before long we were playing almost every night. Our conversations were mainly about strategy, but gradually we learned more about each other. His name was Patrick. He was eighteen. And he only lived a few hours away in Toronto. During one of our talks I asked if he wanted to meet. At first he was reluctant because I don't think he believed I was a girl. But when I visited Toronto with a group of friends, he agreed to meet us at Union Station. I had no idea what he looked like. I just knew he had blonde hair and blue eyes. So when I finally found him, I kinda clammed up. It was like: 'Oh my God, this guy is cute.' We spent hours walking around the city. We went to the top of the CN tower. And after that day, our conversations became much more frequent. We'd have these long MSN chats every night. I'd rush to my computer the moment I got home. It felt nice. To get to talk to someone. Even if it was about my stupid day. Patrick was the first boyfriend I'd ever had— even if our relationship was mostly online. He broke me out of my shell. I wasn't the girl who stared at her shoes anymore. Somebody cared what I had to say. The relationship only lasted seven months. We were so young, and there was no way long distance would work. But my new sense of confidence stayed with me. And several years later, when we reconnected as adults, everything just clicked. We got married in 2017. It wasn't a total gamer wedding. Nobody dressed like elves or anything. But we did play some World of Warcraft tavern music at the reception."

CHAPTER V

A Mutually Assured Attachment

I heard the rumor from a random girl in school. She told me that my boyfriend had gotten another girl pregnant. He'd cheated on me before—so I assumed it was true. But for awhile he denied everything. Then he shifted to blaming the girl. Her name was Stacie. And as the story often goes, I turned all my hatred and hurt toward her. We literally never spoke. And my boyfriend would talk her down every chance he got. I'd occasionally see her when she dropped the baby off at the house. I'd feel such hatred every time the doorbell would ring. She was always so well put-together. There was this unapproachable air about her. Like she was better than everyone else. Worst of all—she had this connection with my boyfriend that I didn't have. The connection of a child. And that was thrown in my face every time she came to the door. My jealousy created a monster inside of me. I withdrew from everyone. Then one year later I got pregnant myself. I didn't feel any excitement. Instead there was a moment of clarity. I couldn't raise a child with this man. He was a pathological liar. For weeks I went back-and-forth. Do I get an abortion? Do I give the child up for adoption? Then one day I made the decision to become a single mother. I remember being so scared. And the first person I thought of was Stacie. It was like: 'My God, I've vilified this woman for so long. And now I'm her. And she is me.' I picked up my phone and sent her a text. I apologized for everything. And I asked for her support. That was eleven years ago. But we still love to joke about how our horrible taste in men when we were young brought us together. Stacie is my best friend in the world. She's my person. Our daughters know each other as sisters. At times she's been my roommate, my biggest confidant, and my maid of honor. Sometimes I think back to those early days, watching her walk up the driveway. I think about all the hatred I would feel. And now it's her hugs that I need when I'm feeling upset. There have been some bad episodes in my life. But every time I'm down, she shows up. The doorbell will ring on a random Tuesday. At 4 PM. And when I open up the door—there she is. And she'll give me the biggest hug."

CHAPTER VI

Hello, Good Bye

I really wish he'd left letters. My sister was relieved, because she didn't want to read it. She knew what a letter would say: 'I love you,' 'You're going to be OK,' and all that stuff. And that's probably true. But still. I wanted to know what mine would say. I wanted one that said: 'Dear Claire.' Maybe there would have been something different. Something just for me. I was the sporty one. In high school I played on his water polo team. And he's the first one I called when my college team won the ultimate frisbee championship. I called him for everything. So many of my friends hated their dads. They wanted nothing to do with them. I used to feel so sorry for them. But now they still have their stupid dads —and I don't. He left nothing behind. No explanation. I learned later that he'd been battling OCD his entire life. Maybe water polo was the thing that kept him grounded. He coached for thirty years. It was his passion. So when he finally retired, and he lost that focus-- his problems became more apparent. Toward the end he stopped sleeping. He was terrified of germs. He thought every little thing was going to kill him. Maybe he was so afraid of death that he couldn't wait anymore. But this is all a guess—he never shared his problems with me. It's like: 'C'mon Dad, we could have talked about it. I'm going to find out eventually if you kill yourself.' He never wanted a funeral, but we hosted a water polo tournament in his honor. The turnout was amazing. People came from all over the country. When it was time for the women's game, I went back to the office to change into my suit. My dad had spent a lot of time in there. In the corner there was a desk that served as a lost and found. It was covered in old goggles and things that nobody wanted to reclaim. Lying on the pile was a slightly rusting necklace, in the shape of a heart. There was a letter C on it. Maybe I should have left it, but I felt like it was for me. I know it's stupid. Usually I roll my eyes at that kind of stuff. But it was a heart. On that day. In that spot. With a letter C. And It just felt like mine to keep. It felt like something that finally said: 'I love you. And you're going to be OK.'"

CHAPTER VII

Swipe of Love

He wasn't my type. He was nerdy. He was wearing Converse. And he talked like a robot. But it had been over a year since anyone had paid attention to me. And I was enjoying our conversation. I never told him that I had a daughter. I just wanted to be 'that girl at the brewery.' For one afternoon, I didn't want to be the young, single mother. And it was nice. It was nice to feel wanted again. When he asked if we could go out sometime, I didn't even hesitate. But I started feeling nervous as soon as I got home. Because I started thinking about all the places a date could lead, and I knew I had to tell him. So I sent him a text. It said: 'You should know I have a daughter. Things aren't good with her father. I'm not asking you to fill that role, but if you want to cancel the date-- we can.' There were twenty minutes of silence. And then he replied: 'It is what it is.' Just like a robot. Then he wrote: 'If the date sucks, we never have to talk again.' We made plans to meet at a famous brunch place. They didn't even serve alcohol, which made everything twice as awkward. We agreed to take it slow. And to just have fun with things. He made it very clear that he wasn't in a place where he wanted to be a dad. And that remained his official stance for about three months, until he met her. It's been over two years now. So he's been there her entire life. They're obsessed with each other. She constantly wants to talk with him about everything. She wants me to call him when she farts. She wants to be a Wildcat fan because he went to Arizona. And when we find a shell on the beach, she'll pick it up. But it's always for him—not me. And he loves that little girl. But that's not surprising. What's surprising is that he loves me. Roo is easy to love. She's so young. She doesn't withdraw or want space. She doesn't have scars. She's never been abandoned. She accepts love without question, and she gives it without question. They love each other so much. So much that it makes me nervous. Sometimes I'll ask him: 'Do you just love me because you don't want to lose her?' And he'll say: 'No. I love her a ton, and I love you a ton.' He always says it very calmly. Just like a robot."

CHAPTER VIII

Nutty and Nice

Alex's father left for good when he was eighteen months old. I was doing the single mother stuff. Working at a daycare. Home all the time. Trying to be a really great mom while also trying to fix myself. I remember the first Christmas I spent alone. I was finally in a good place. I was still hurting, but I didn't want him back anymore. And that New Year's Eve was the first time I met Jose. He was a friend of my brother's. We started talking every day. He'd come over for dinner. I think he was tentative around Alex at first. He'd get on the floor and try playing with him, but Alex couldn't speak yet. So there wasn't much of a bond. Then the 'terrible twos' came. And Alex would throw a lot of tantrums. Jose hadn't been around kids before, and he didn't want to overstep. I think he was unsure of his role. But after he decided to move in with us, I told him: 'I want you to make more of an effort with Alex. He's part of me.' And that's exactly what he did. He didn't always know exactly what to do. But he brought home diapers and milk, even when nobody asked. He played cops and robbers, and nerf guns, and video games. He came to the parent teacher conferences. That year our whole family went to the Christmas play at Alex's school. And after the performance, when everyone was taking pictures, a classmate asked Alex where his dad was. And he pointed at Jose. I was the only one who saw it. But when I told Jose later, I could tell that it affected him. Alex still believes that Jose is his dad. And I'm dreading when I have to tell him the truth. They're so attached to each other. Jose is not the most emotional guy. But whenever Alex asks for a hug or a kiss, he'll always give it to him. Even if it's twenty times a day. He's always saying: 'I love you too, Papa.' That's just how he is. He reciprocates. He's rarely the first one to express his emotions. But a few months ago we were having breakfast. And somehow Alex found a picture of me holding him at the hospital—right after he was born. He carried it over to Jose, and asked: 'Where are you? Did you take this picture?' Jose looked at it, and he started crying. Then he said: 'Yes, Papa. I did.'"

CHAPTER IX

Hop,Skip,Wed

I was married once before. It was a 300-person wedding in a massive Catholic church. With a big, grand dress that cost $1400. It was a fairy tale dream and I thought it was perfect. But within a year, things started to feel off. He became increasingly critical of me. And I found myself getting more and more subdued. Then a year into our marriage, he told me that he was having an affair. Suddenly I was thrown back into the whole dating thing. It was like: 'Oh no. Not this again.' But a few years later I met Thylar on an app, and right away things felt different. He accepted things about me that had been rejected in the past. Superficial stuff-- like TV shows and movies and bands. If I wanted to put a Dr. Who decal on my car, he wouldn't question it. He was even more eccentric than me. Thylar is obsessed with a convenience store called Buccee's. Their mascot is a beaver. He loves that beaver. He has like twenty mugs with that beaver on it. Both of us were coming from a similar place. We'd both dealt with infidelity in the past, so neither of us were in a rush to get married. We enjoyed taking things day-by-day. And we went on like that for two years, until one morning I woke up to the sound of Thylar groaning. He was kicking his right leg into the air. When I called 911, the dispatcher told me he was having a stroke. I rode with him in the back of the ambulance. He kept pointing at his eyes, then his chest, then at me. He began squeezing my ring finger, and tapping it. I knew what he was trying to say, but I just chalked it up to panic. Even after his recovery, I never brought it up. Because I didn't want him to feel pressured. The next summer we held a live music benefit for his medical bills. After the third song, Thylar walked up to the microphone. He told everyone that he'd learned a lot from his experience. And that if you find a bright spot in this world-- you should hang onto it. Then he proposed to me in front of all our friends and family. We were married two months later. It was a spot where we loved to go hiking. Far off the trail, deep in the woods, beneath some great arching trees. There were only two witnesses. And I wore a $75 dress."

CHAPTER X

One and Only

We were together for three years. He wasn't a bad person. He worked hard. He was charismatic. But he was hiding a major drug problem from me. There were violent episodes. He once choked me in a hotel room while we were on vacation. He broke my phone. He tried to rip up my passport. Then on the way home, he dropped to one knee in the airport and asked me to marry him. That was the pattern. We'd get in a huge fight, then after a few days he'd 'love bomb' me. He'd say that he needed me. And that he'd never get better without me. So I'd take him back, and the cycle would begin all over again. One Monday morning there was a knock on our door. It was my mother, and she told me that my sister had been pulled over by the police. She was battling a drug addiction of her own. They found empty needles all over her car, and my two-year-old nephew Robert was placed into foster care. From that moment on—all I could think about was getting him back. But it was nearly impossible. I had to complete an eight-week certification course. I had to rent a two-bedroom apartment in San Francisco, which I couldn't even afford. And everyone living with me had to pass a background check. I knew that my boyfriend had a misdemeanor for domestic violence. So I had to make a decision: him or Robert. And I chose Robert. I officially became his foster parent in October of 2018. Ever since then I've been focused on his healing. He can't verbalize yet. Sometimes he has tantrums and I just need to hold him tight. He's been through a lot of trauma-- so he needs me. But I needed him too. I'd still be stuck in the cycle if it wasn't for Robert. I didn't know who I was anymore. I needed to learn to be alone. I needed to learn that chaos wasn't normal. The last two years haven't been easy. The whole family is chipping in. My mom is working two jobs to help with rent. Everyone is under a lot of stress. But it's a lot of peace too. I'm not walking around on eggshells anymore. I'm not terrified of being alone. I'm enjoying my solitude. Last June I got baptized, and I feel like I'm becoming a new person. My life has a purpose now. Robert's adoption went through on March 10th. So I'm officially his mother."

ACKNOWLEDGEMENT

To my wonderful readers:I love you guys.

ABOUT THE AUTHOR

Kim Matos

For the past undisclosed amount of years, Kim Matos has been freelancing and designing blogs for small businesses.She lives in northern california with her dead fish larry and a bouncy bunny rabbit named Fred.

When she is not writting,she can be found picking up trash off the beaches,offering rides to the homeless and roastting her own coffee beans.

BOOKS BY THIS AUTHOR

Cougar Husband And Other Stories

This book is an interesting love story about a woman who never knew the true identity of the man he married and other stories.

CONTACT ME

Click here to join my Reader's group and your free book "COUGAR HUSBAND AND OTHER STORIES" - It will be delivered to your inbox.You will also be kept up to date about other give-aways coming up soon.